E
NOL

The Lizard Man
of Crabtree County

by Lucy Nolan • illustrated by Jill Kastner

MARSHALL CAVENDISH   NEW YORK

Marshall Cavendish, 99 White Plains Road, Tarrytown, NY 10591

Library of Congress Cataloging–in–Publication Data
Nolan, Lucy A.
The Lizard Man of Crabtree County / by Lucy Nolan: illustrations by Jill Kastner.
p.   cm. Summary: James becomes the unwitting source of wild rumors that a
Lizard Man has appeared in his quiet rural community.
ISBN 0-7614-5144-7 [1. Monsters–Fiction. 2. Country life–Fiction.] I. Kastner, Jill, ill.
II. Title.   PZ7.N688Li   1999   [Fic]–dc21   98–47938   CIP   AC

The text of this book is set in 16 point Nofret Medium.
The illustrations are rendered in oils on paper.
1 2 3 4 5 6   Printed in Hong Kong. First Marshall Cavendish Paperbacks Edition 2003

To Edward Nolan
and in loving memory of
Margaret Nolan
—L. N.

For Katie,
who asked for a book
—J. K.

Welcome to
Crabtree County
Population 376
Home of the
Lincoln Squash!

Exciting things don't happen very often in Crabtree County.

Oh, every now and then Farmer French's cow gets loose
and chases cars.
And once, someone grew a squash that looked like
Abraham Lincoln.
But other than that, things are pretty quiet.

   That's why everyone got all shaken-up the summer
the Lizard Man appeared.

It all started the very same day that James Arthur decided to be a shrub. If he looked like a shrub, maybe something interesting would happen. A bird might land on his head. Or maybe he could sneak up on a rabbit.

Anyway, he plastered leaves all over himself and acted like a bush.

But by the end of the day, absolutely nothing exciting had happened.

Well, that wasn't quite true. James Arthur did manage to fool a family of bugs into thinking he was a plant. But now those bugs were making a home in his underwear.

James Arthur hurried down the path to rinse off in Miss Bunch's pond.

When James Arthur got home, his mother was just hanging up the telephone.

"Well, that's the strangest thing I've ever heard," she said. "Miss Bunch just saw a giant Lizard Man, with green scales and big claws and a pointy head. He was heading straight for her pond."

"Wow!" James Arthur cried. "I was just there. The Lizard Man could have eaten me!"

Finally, something exciting was happening in Crabtree County.

The next day, James Arthur was up early. He ate
a big breakfast. He called to his beagle, Moondog.
Then he strapped on his handy–dandy,
super–duper Lizard Man tracking gear.

His mother told him not to go in the water.

No fair! He was sure the Lizard Man lived down
where the mud got all slimy and gooey.

James Arthur stood on the shore and threw
breadcrumbs. This attracted a flock of ducks and
one very cranky goose. But no Lizard Man. When
Moondog ate the rest of the bread, James Arthur
went home.

That evening, James Arthur's father had exciting news. The volunteer fire department had just gone to Miss Bunch's pond to look for the Lizard Man. They found some very large, very creepy tracks that went 'round and 'round the pond.

The next day, James Arthur decided to wait until after supper to start his Lizard Man hunt.

It was getting awfully late, and James Arthur was ready to go home, when he suddenly heard footsteps. He sat very still. The hair stood up on the back of his neck.

At that very moment, the moon appeared over the treetops and Moondog threw back his head and howled.

The footsteps stopped. Then they ran the other way. James Arthur didn't know lizard feet could make so much noise.

"No fair!" James Arthur told Moondog. "You scared him away."

The next day, the county was in an uproar. The firemen had gone back to Miss Bunch's pond the night before. The Lizard Man chased them. He had a terrible, horrible, spine-tingling wail.

No fair! James Arthur wanted to hear the Lizard Man.

He would sleep in a tree all night if he had to. And he wasn't taking Moondog.

That night, James Arthur sneaked out of the house. He sat in an old hollow tree. Then he learned something important.

Other things sit in old hollow trees, too.

James Arthur decided this wasn't such a good idea after all.

The next morning, the county was buzzing with news. It seemed that the Lizard Man had eaten one of Miss Bunch's chickens.

"What will he do next?" James Arthur wondered.

This Lizard Man was tricky. But James Arthur managed to come up with one more clever plan to catch him.

Maybe he could attract the Lizard Man with a Lizard Woman. James Arthur put a bow on his Sammy-the-Sea-Serpent float and headed back to the pond.

He waited all day, but the Lizard Man never came.

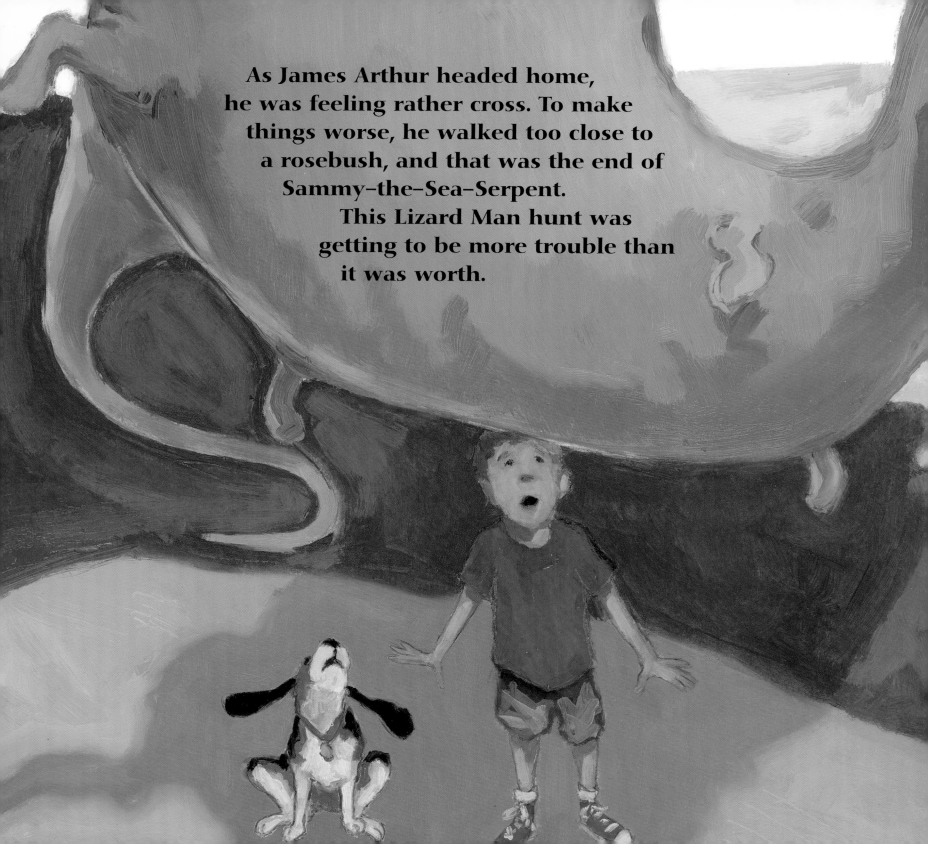

As James Arthur headed home,
he was feeling rather cross. To make
things worse, he walked too close to
a rosebush, and that was the end of
Sammy-the-Sea-Serpent.
This Lizard Man hunt was
getting to be more trouble than
it was worth.

When James Arthur got home, his mother hung up the telephone.

"Good news! Miss Bunch says the Lizard Man is gone. He just jumped on a truck heading for Alabama."

The news quickly spread. Everyone in Crabtree County felt much better. Except for James Arthur. He sat and pouted.

No fair! Something exciting had finally happened in Crabtree County, . . .

. . . and James Arthur never saw a thing.